At The
Going
Of The
Of The
And In
The Me

Down

Sun

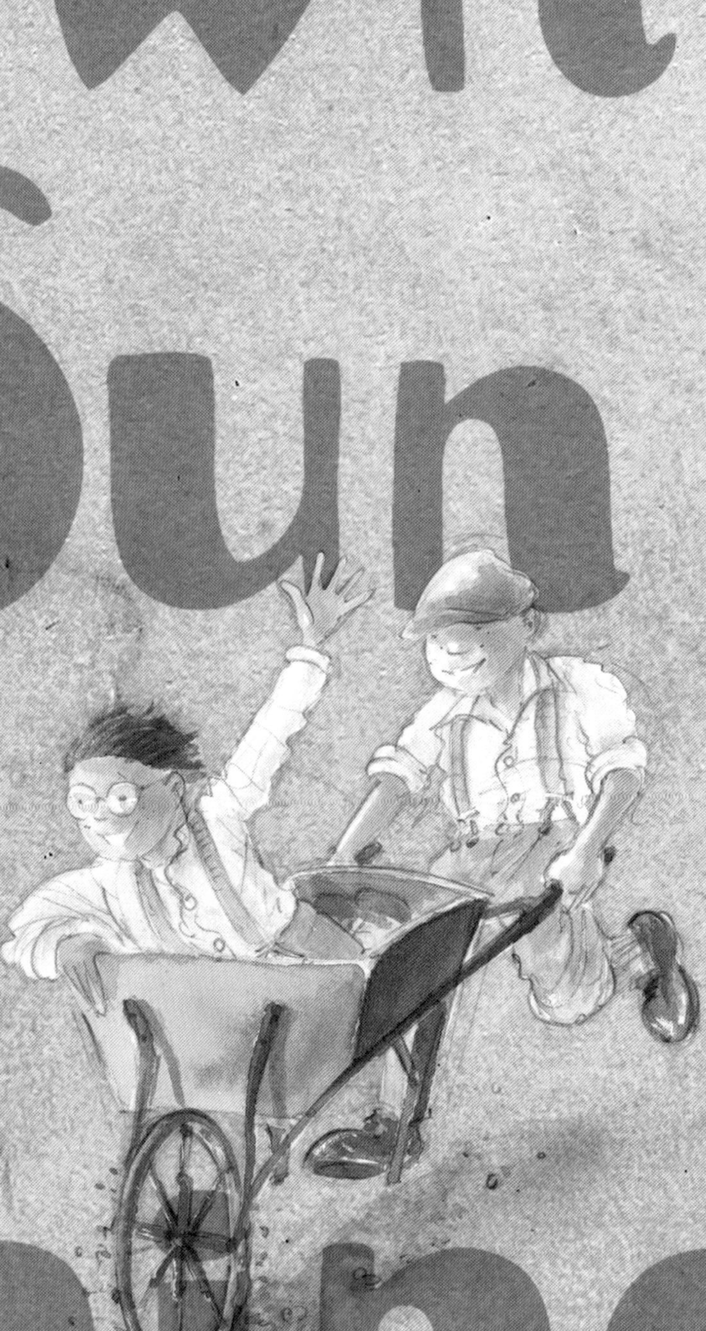

rning

Serjeant
George B N Johnson
13th Battalion, Rifle Brigade.
Fell at the Battle of the Somme 10th July 1916
Age 22

HR

Rifleman
Arthur James Sainty
1/5th Battalion, London Rifle Brigade.
Fell at the Battle of the Somme 9th October 1916
Age 19

MI

"Here sleep the gentlemen with black buttons."
Lt. Gen. Sir Henry F. M. Wilson

first edition March 2014
reprinted June 2014

STRAUSS HOUSE PRODUCTIONS
Lumby Grange, Lumby, South Milford, North Yorkshire, LS25 5JA
www.strausshouseproductions.com

Where The Poppies Now Grow

by
Hilary Robinson and Martin Impey

STRAUSS HOUSE
PRODUCTIONS

This is the field where the poppies now grow.

These are the children who like to play
Out in the field where the poppies now grow.

This is Ben and his best friend Ray
Who are two of the children that like to play
Out in the field where the poppies now grow.

These are the trenches used for cover
To hide from the enemy and each other,
Built by Ben and his best friend Ray
Who are two of the children that like to play
Out in the field where the poppies now grow.

This is the makeshift aerodrome
With barricades of sand and stone
That shield the trenches used for cover,
To hide from the enemy and each other
Built by Ben and his best friend Ray
Who are two of the children that like to play
Out in the field where the poppies now grow.

These are the armies joined up by men,
Men like Ray and his old friend Ben
Who march by the makeshift aerodrome
With barricades of sand and stone
That shield the trenches used for cover
To hide from the enemy and each other,
Built by Ben and his best friend Ray
Who were two of the children that liked to play
Out in the field where the poppies now grow.

This is the battlefield, barren and stark
A stage for a war, dangerous and dark,
To be charged by armies joined up by men,
Men like Ray and his old friend Ben
Who march by the makeshift aerodrome
With barricades of sand and stone
That shield the trenches used for cover
To hide from the enemy and each other,
Built by Ben and his best friend Ray
Who were two of the children that liked to play
Out in the field where the poppies now grow.

This is the soldier, injured and hurt
Left to die in the cold and the dirt
Out on the battlefield, barren and stark
That staged a war, dangerous and dark,
Charged on by armies joined up by men,
Men like Ray and his old friend Ben
Who march by the makeshift aerodrome
With barricades of sand and stone
That shield the trenches used for cover
To hide from the enemy and each other,
Built by Ben and his best friend Ray
Who were two of the children that liked to play
Out in the field where the poppies now grow.

This is the soldier, bold and brave
Who risked his life in order to save
Another soldier, injured and hurt
Left to die in the cold and the dirt
Out on the battlefield, barren and stark
That staged a war, dangerous and dark,
Charged on by armies joined up by men,
Men like Ray and his old friend Ben
Who march by the makeshift aerodrome
With barricades of sand and stone
That shield the trenches used for cover
To hide from the enemy and each other,
Built by Ben and his best friend Ray
Who were two of the children that liked to play
Out in the field where the poppies now grow.

Ben was the soldier Ray found.

Ben was the soldier Ray found
Lying alone on the battleground.
Ray was the soldier, bold and brave
Who risked his life in order to save
Another soldier, injured and hurt
Left to die in the cold and the dirt
Out on the battlefield, barren and stark
That staged a war, dangerous and dark,
Charged on by armies joined up by men,
Men like Ray and his old friend Ben
Who marched by the makeshift aerodrome
And barricades of sand and stone
That shielded the trenches used for cover
To hide from the enemy and each other,
Built by Ben and his best friend Ray
Who were two of the children that liked to play
Out in the field...

...where the poppies now grow.

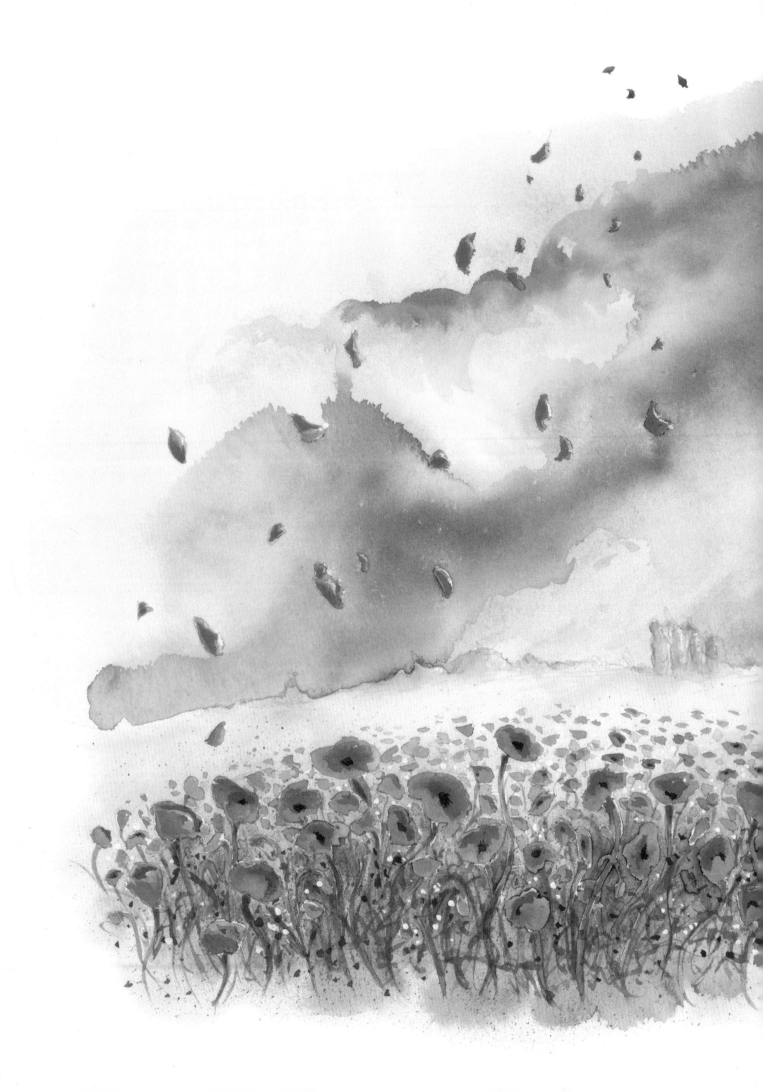

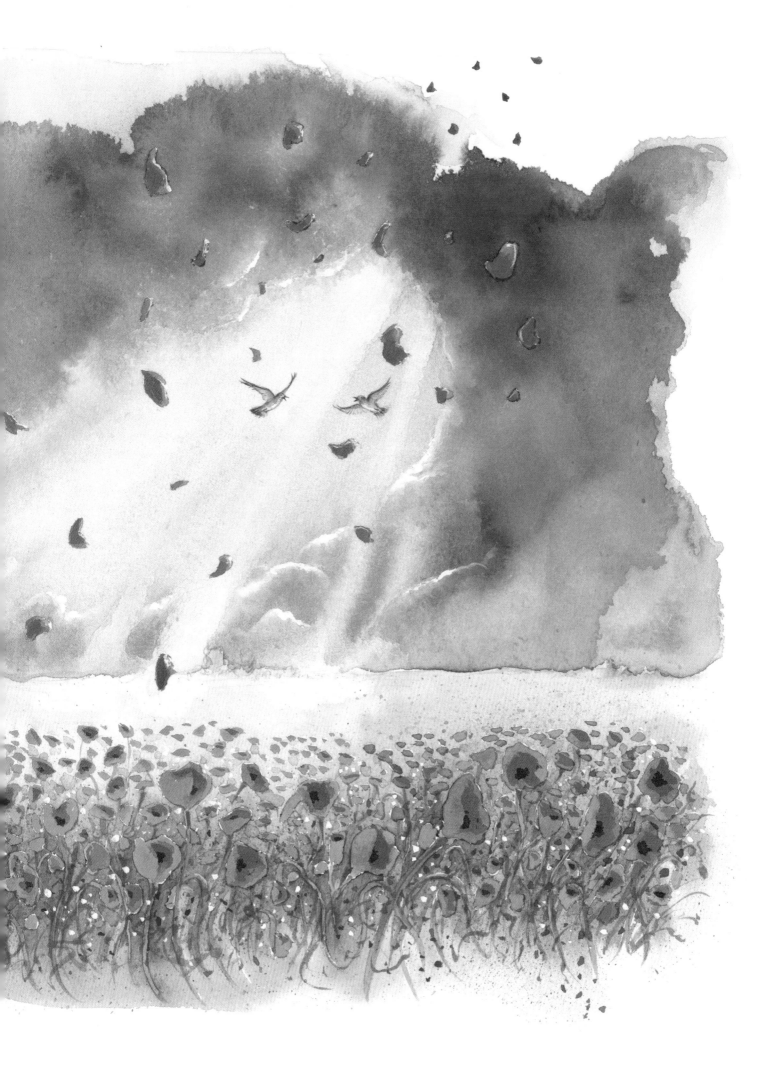

We Wi
Remem
Them

Thank you

Jackie Hamley,
Jim Millea, Roy Player, Chris Lowe, Dominic Walker,
Robert Prizeman, Gary Brandham, Keith Collman,
Nicky Stonehill, Jessica Ward, Matthew Ward, Gill Fraser Lee,
Paul Reed, Joke De Winter and Megan Brownrigg.

This poppy is for you.
It is a symbol of remembrance.
Please dedicate it to the memory of a family member, or friend,
who devoted their life to the cause of peace.

By writing a name here,
their memory will live on in all those who read this copy of
Where The Poppies Now Grow.

Also by
Hilary Robinson & Martin Impey

The Christmas Truce
The Place Where Peace Was Found

by
Hilary Robinson & Martin Impey

ISBN - 978-0-9571245-7-8